# a FRieNDSHiP to RemembeR

by Perdita Finn

Little, Brown and Company
New York * Boston

HASBRO and its logo, MY LITTLE PONY, EQUESTRIA GIRLS and all related characters are trademarks of Hasbro and are used with permission. © 2017 Hasbro. All Rights Reserved.

Cover design by Véronique L. Sweet.

Little, Brown and Company
Hachette Book Group
1290 Avenue of the Americas, New York, NY 10104
Visit us at LBYR.com
MLPEG.com

First Edition: December 2017

Little, Brown and Company is a division of Hachette Book Group, Inc. The Little, Brown name and logo are trademarks of Hachette Book Group, Inc.

The publisher is not responsible for websites (or their content) that are not owned by the publisher.

Library of Congress Control Number 2017946351

ISBNs: 978-0-316-55735-1 (paper over board), 978-0-316-55732-0 (ebook)

Printed in the United States of America

LSC-H

10 9 8 7 6 5 4 3 2 1

For Ella

# CONTENTS

$\star$ $\star$ $\star$

CHAPTER 1

# A Friendship to Remember

# ✷ ✶ ✷

Sunset Shimmer grabbed her camera from her locker. As the editor of Canterlot High's yearbook, she always had to be ready to capture a special memory. Her friends were bustling down the hallway to class. She wanted to take pictures of them all. Twilight Sparkle and Applejack called out a greeting as they passed. Sunset Shimmer snapped a photo. Fluttershy caught her eye and smiled at her sweetly. Sunset Shimmer clicked her camera again. It was another great shot. This would be the best yearbook ever!

She had to make sure there were lots of candid photos. She also had to get a photo of every club and every team—and there were so many of them! Once she finished taking the photos, the whole school needed to vote on Superlatives, and then she had to arrange and lay out the pictures of the Best Dressed and the Most Talented. She wondered who would win in the Best Friends category this year. She knew whom she was voting for.

Rainbow Dash came over to say hello and posed for a photo. Just as Sunset Shimmer raised her camera, she saw Pinkie Pie sneak up behind Rainbow Dash. Pinkie winked as she held up bunny ears behind Rainbow Dash's head. Sunset Shimmer snapped the photo, trying not to giggle. Rainbow Dash whirled around when she realized Pinkie was behind her and laughed out loud. All the girls crowded around Sunset Shimmer to look at the photo. It would be so funny and cute in the yearbook.

So much had changed for Sunset Shimmer. When she first came to Canterlot High from Equestria, the magical land of ponies, she had wanted to be the queen bee. But instead of becoming the most popular girl in the whole school, she had terrified everyone by turning into a she-demon. Luckily, Princess Twilight had come from Equestria just in time to stop her path of destruction.

Best of all, the very girls to whom she'd been meanest had forgiven her. They had even started hanging out with her. Since then, Sunset Shimmer had been learning about the most powerful magic of all—friendship. She used to think she was tough, but she was really just lonely. She never wanted to be all alone ever again.

All day long, Sunset Shimmer took photos of her friends. She knew she would always treasure them. She captured Twilight Sparkle studying hard in the library. She took a picture of all the girls posing by Applejack's shiny red pickup truck. She never wanted to forget all their wonderful adventures together—from winning the Friendship Games to saving Camp Everfree and discovering the crystal geodes that gave each girl her own special magic.

That afternoon, they all met in the yearbook office to begin laying out the pages. Their geodes glowed. Twilight Sparkle used her special telekinesis to upload Sunset Shimmer's camera's memory card. Rainbow Dash zoomed around the room at lightning speed from workstation to workstation. Applejack used her super strength to lift a heavy printer and move it from one table to another. All around the girls, magic sparkled...but the best magic of all was how easily and happily they worked together. Sunset Shimmer never took it for granted.

"I want to treasure these memories forever," she confided to the other girls.

"We all do," agreed Twilight Sparkle. "We'll always be able to look through our yearbooks and remember how much our friendship meant to us."

"Best friends forever," Pinkie exclaimed. "Forever and ever and ever."

"Forever," Sunset Shimmer repeated. She and her friends would never, ever forget one another. Would they?

CHAPTER 2

# The Queen
# of Clubs

# ✦ ✦ ✦

Sunset Shimmer looked over her schedule for the yearbook. She had to find a way to photograph all the after-school activities in a single afternoon. Could she do it? She would have to move fast. Hopefully nothing would go wrong....Like seeing one of her best friends walk through the front door of the high school with a giant pig. But that's just what Sunset Shimmer saw that morning as Applejack tugged a plump pig through the hall on a leash. Oh no! What was Applejack doing? Sunset Shimmer rushed over to find out. The pig grunted before plopping down in the middle of the hallway. Applejack yanked on his leash, but he wouldn't budge. She laughed.

Rarity stared at the pig, wrinkling her nose.

"Why did you bring a pig to school, Applejack?" Sunset Shimmer asked her friend. "Today of all days!"

"It's photo day for all the clubs!" Applejack explained.

"Exactly!" exclaimed Sunset Shimmer.

"And it's a Young Farmers' Club tradition to have your critter in the yearbook picture."

*"Awww!"* gushed Fluttershy, coming over

to pat the pig. He snorted and blinked his long-lashed eyes.

What could Sunset Shimmer say? She hadn't thought about the animals that needed to have their photos taken. She looked over her schedule.

"You're lucky you're in only *one* club," said Rainbow Dash to Applejack. "I'm in five this year. *So* busy."

Applejack looked concerned. "Young Farmers' is just one of the *six* clubs I'm in."

Rainbow Dash shook her head, not impressed. "I meant five *sports* clubs."

"Darlings, please!" Rarity stepped in to make peace. "It's not a competition."

"Actually it is," piped up Sunset Shimmer. "The yearbook always has a special photo of the Most Involved student, only I haven't figured out who that is yet."

Rainbow Dash grinned. Applejack's eyes lit up. A competition. Rainbow Dash and Applejack liked nothing more than competition. They studied each other. Who was in more clubs? Who *could* be in more clubs? Who would win the prize for Most Involved when the yearbook came out?

That afternoon, Rainbow Dash raced from one meeting to another. She sped into the library; crashed into Sunset Shimmer, who was just setting up the photo; and studied a chessboard for less than a second, moved a piece, grinned, and dashed out. She had to get to her next club!

At another table in the library, Applejack played Ogres and Oubliettes with Trixie and a bunch of other kids. They studied the board, a giant map covered in figurines. Everyone wore a silly hat—except

Applejack, who had on a football helmet. She clearly didn't fit in, especially since her pig sat beside her. But that didn't matter. She would get her picture in the yearbook no matter what!

Sunset Shimmer clicked her camera. She looked at her photo. Not so good— except for the pig. He was actually quite photogenic. She took another photo of the game players.

Meanwhile, Rainbow Dash had joined Fluttershy's knitting circle. The girls sat on the steps of the school with balls of yarn. Their needles flashed in the sun. Rainbow Dash picked up a pair and knitted super fast. In under a minute she held up a tiny sweater with a design of the Canterlot High Wondercolt. Fluttershy clapped her hands, delighted, and put it on her pet bunny.

Sunset Shimmer snapped a photo for the yearbook. What a moment to treasure.

But Applejack and Rainbow Dash didn't have time to treasure anything. They were too busy racing from club to club. Applejack showed up in the gym, ready to have her picture taken with the Fencing Club. They all stood on a mat wearing their fencing gear—masks on their faces and swords in their hands. Applejack was confused. She had brought a piece of the fence from her farm! Still, she jumped into the photo anyway, pulling her pig behind her. She'd put a lot of effort into fixing that fence. Why couldn't she be in the Fencing Club?

"Is there any rule against it?" Applejack asked Sunset Shimmer. Her pig grunted happily beside her.

"Nope," she answered, taking a moment

to catch her breath. She wasn't in any club except Yearbook, but that one club kept her busier than all of them combined! Putting together a yearbook took a lot of work.

As soon as the photo shoot was over, Applejack raced across the gym to where the cheerleaders were meeting. They all formed a pyramid. But Applejack touched her sparkling geode necklace and activated her super strength. She was going to lift all the cheerleaders into the air! She did it with one hand, her pig standing right beside her. Her pig smiled, the star of the photo shoot yet again. That would be an amazing picture—and it was!

Sunset Shimmer heard a huge explosion in the distance. It sounded like an experiment gone wrong.

"The Science Club!" she said. She had to get there fast.

Applejack and her pig raced down the hallway beside her. "Cooking is a kind of science," said Applejack breathlessly. "And I'm great at cookin'. This'll be another great club for me."

But Rainbow Dash had already beaten her to it. Twilight Sparkle shook her head as Rainbow Dash held up a smoking test tube. *Oops!* She had soot all over her face. But Sunset Shimmer had somehow managed to capture it all. It would be in the yearbook—another memory of her friends and how creative and wonderful they were.

But Applejack frowned and counted on her fingers. Did Rainbow Dash have more clubs than she did now? Maybe.

Rainbow Dash took off down the hall and whizzed into the art room. She picked up a paintbrush and splattered some colors across a canvas. She wasn't half bad! She glanced out the window as the marching band passed by, practicing. Oh no! Applejack was clanging a triangle. She had joined that club, too! Rainbow Dash would have to find another club to keep up with her. Were there any left?

Sunset Shimmer leaned against the wall and looked back over her photos. Art Club. Check. Marching band. Check. Somehow she had kept up with her busy friends—and so had the pig. Now who was in the most clubs? It was time to tally the score.

The bell rang. All after-school activities were now over.

Exhausted, Rainbow Dash collapsed on

the front lawn. Applejack and her pig joined her. They both grinned at each other. That had been fun! Who had won?

Sunset Shimmer joined them, camera in hand. She was tired, too. She wiped some sweat from her forehead. "Well, the scores are in," she began, looking at a paper in her hand.

Applejack, looking over her shoulder, couldn't believe it! "It's a darn tootin' tie!"

"You have got to be kidding me!" Rainbow Dash said with a laugh. "After all that?"

"At least between the two of us, we joined every club at Canterlot High," noted Applejack. That was an achievement.

Rarity cleared her throat. She had joined them and sat down beside Applejack's pig. "Not all the clubs," she said smugly.

Applejack and Rainbow Dash looked confused.

Rarity had Sunset Shimmer scroll down the photos on her camera to a glamour shot of Rarity all by herself.

What club was this? Was it about fashion or celebrity? Could they join?

Rarity laughed. "Oh no, darlings. It's very exclusive."

Applejack studied the picture. In the background, she noticed her pig! What was he doing in the photo? "Is that my pig?"

"Well, of course!" Rarity exclaimed. "You can't expect me to be the president *and* the vice president. And he's not really so smelly once he's wearing a little perfume."

Sunset Shimmer shook her head, looking through the photos on her camera.

"Your pig is the real winner," she told Applejack. "He's in more clubs than anyone!"

Everyone laughed, and the pig grunted happily.

Sunset Shimmer was the happiest of all. Her friends were so energetic and involved and funny. Every day was an adventure with them, and she never wanted to forget a single moment they had shared. Thanks to the yearbook, she wouldn't have to. That was for sure.

CHAPTER

3

# Super Superlatives

★ ✦ ★

Sunset Shimmer was directing Twilight Sparkle and Applejack as they arranged photos in the yearbook room. They had to be carefully cropped to fit into the layout. Sunset Shimmer was really happy with the way the yearbook was beginning to look. That's because they were working on it as a team.

"I remember when I didn't have any friends," Sunset Shimmer said to the others. "But you all forgave me for stealing the magic crown."

"Of course we did!" said Applejack. "And since then, we have had a lotta good times together. Remember when we found our magic gems?" She touched the geode around her neck.

"How could I ever forget!" exclaimed Sunset Shimmer. She clapped her hands and accidentally bumped into a girl she hadn't noticed before in the yearbook office. "Oops!"

"Excuse me," whispered the girl.

"I'm sorry," Sunset Shimmer apologized. "I didn't see you come in."

The girl bit her lip, looking down at the floor shyly. "I've been here awhile," she murmured.

"I didn't realize—"

"I've been trying to get your attention," she interrupted.

"Ain't she a quiet one?" noted Applejack softly.

"Yeah," agreed Rainbow Dash. "And we know some pretty shy people, am I right?" She looked at Fluttershy, who blushed.

"I'm Sunset Shimmer," she said to the new girl. "President of the Yearbook Committee and editor in chief. Do you want to join? We could always use extra help."

"I'm Wallflower," answered the girl, still not meeting her eyes.

"Nice to meet you," answered Sunset Shimmer.

"I've been on the Yearbook Committee all year," Wallflower said quietly.

Sunset Shimmer felt terrible. "Oh! *Umm...*"

"We've had literally dozens of classes together since we met in ninth-grade English." Wallflower looked like she was about to cry.

"I—I meant," stammered Sunset Shimmer. "It was nice to meet you then, which is when I also remember us meeting."

Twilight breathed a sigh of relief. Nice save!

"Anyway," Wallflower said with a sigh, "I counted up all the votes for the yearbook Superlatives." She handed Sunset Shimmer a piece of paper. Superlatives were when all the students in the school voted on which kids they thought were best at all different kinds of things. Whoever won got his or her picture taken and had a special page in the yearbook.

Sunset Shimmer read the Superlatives out loud. "Most Likely to Succeed, Best Smile, Class Clown." Her face broke into a big smile, and she held up the paper for the other girls to see. "Look who won Best Friends!" There were all their names—Applejack, Fluttershy, Rainbow Dash, Rarity, Pinkie Pie, Twilight Sparkle, and Sunset Shimmer. Sunset Shimmer's heart felt so happy. Nothing meant more to her than this.

Pinkie Pie clapped her hands, delighted. "I always knew I liked you all, but now it's official! In yearbook form. The people have spoken!"

Twilight looked at some of the other categories on the list. "Oh, good for Micro Chips," she noted a little unhappily. "Most Likely to Invent Cold Fusion."

"Don't be jealous, Twilight," said Fluttershy encouragingly. "We all know you are a genius, too."

"Besides," Rainbow Dash added, "it's just the yearbook."

The other girls gasped.

"Now ya dunnit," whispered Applejack, shaking her head.

*"Just the yearbook?"* Sunset Shimmer was crestfallen. "The student body has entrusted me with the responsibility of gathering memories into the pages of this book. In thirty years, we might not remember everything, but we *will* remember what's in the yearbook."

Wallflower was particularly affected by her words. She looked like she would cry again. "If I'm not in it, would that mean I didn't exist?" Wallflower tried to smile. "Hey, just kidding."

But she spoke so quietly that the other girls didn't even hear her. They were all focused on Sunset Shimmer.

"And now thanks to everyone voting for us, we'll always remember that we're Best Friends," Sunset Shimmer announced.

"And who got Best Muscles." Rainbow Dash smiled and pointed at the sheet. "I'm entrusting you not to put our picture opposite that page. Every time you close the book, it'll be like we're kissing Bulk Biceps!"

The girls laughed out loud. That would be terrible!

"Speaking of photography," announced Rarity. "Why don't we take our picture at the beach Saturday? The lighting will be absolutely to die for!"

"Beach day!" squealed Pinkie. "I'll make my world-famous fun-in-the-sun cupcakes."

Fluttershy's eyes widened. That sounded yummy!

"The secret ingredient," Pinkie whispered to Fluttershy, "is edible sunscreen! It's SPF delicious!"

Fluttershy's face fell. That sounded yucky!

The door to the yearbook office flew open. It was Trixie, and she was furious about something. "The Great and Powerful Trixie demands to speak to the yearbook editor immediately!"

Sunset Shimmer stepped forward reluctantly. "Unfortunately for me, that's me. What do you want, Trixie?"

Trixie snatched the list of Superlatives from her hand and studied it. "Just as I suspected. I was not voted Greatest and Most Powerful! Explain yourself!"

*"Hmmm,"* said Sunset Shimmer, thinking. "How should I put this? You didn't win Greatest and Most Powerful because it wasn't one of the categories."

Trixie flounced right past Sunset Shimmer and pulled an older yearbook from the shelf. She turned to the Superlatives.

"Neither was Biggest Meanie, but that didn't stop you from winning it our freshman year." She held up the yearbook with a picture of Sunset Shimmer. She was scowling and looked like she was about to hit the photographer.

Seeing the picture reminded Sunset Shimmer of all the mistakes she had made. She felt terrible, but she tried to stay calm. That was a long time ago. A lot of wonderful things had happened since then. "That was different."

Applejack jumped in. "Yeah. Sunset Shimmer was so mean that the *whole* school did a write-in vote."

"The editor had no choice but to make it official," agreed Rarity.

"Sunset won Biggest Meanie fair and square," Rainbow Dash told Trixie.

"*Mmm-hmm,*" agreed Fluttershy.

"She was *soooo* mean, remember?" said Pinkie. None of the girls realized how much their memories were affecting Sunset Shimmer... until it was too late.

Sunset Shimmer's face was red with embarrassment. She took a deep breath. "I hope I've earned the right not to be remembered that way."

"Of course!" said Twilight Sparkle reassuringly. "We all know that you've changed, Sunset."

Sunset Shimmer tossed the yearbook aside. "In any case," she said to Trixie, "we're not having a Greatest and Most Powerful Superlative. Sorry."

"You're the one who'll be sorry," fumed Trixie, her eyes narrowing. "When you least expect it, I'll have my revenge, and then I'll disappear....Like *this*!" She waved her arms dramatically. "Behold! The Magician's Exit!"

Trixie threw a smoke bomb into the middle of the room! *Poof!* But when the smoke cleared, Trixie was still there, jiggling the handle of the door out of the yearbook room. She couldn't get it open.

"Allow me," said Sunset Shimmer, flicking the lock. "We were actually on our way out."

Trixie stormed out in front of her, and the girls all burst out laughing as they left. Sunset Shimmer hit the lights.

From the darkness came a small, quiet voice. "Oh, I was still in here. But that's okay. I'm used to it."

Nobody saw Wallflower leave all by herself, the old yearbook under her arm.

CHAPTER

4

# Most Changed

★ ★ ★

Sunset Shimmer was tucked into bed, writing in her magic journal. Long before she came to Canterlot High, she had lived in Equestria. For each of her friends now, there was a pony just like her, and with the same name in that enchanted world. She'd even befriended Twilight Sparkle, the counterpart for her friend Princess Twilight, the pony who knew everything about friendship—and who had rescued her when she had turned into a she-demon. Sunset Shimmer still kept in touch with Princess Twilight. Whatever she wrote in her journal would magically appear in Twilight's own diary in Equestria.

*Dear Princess Twilight,* she wrote. *I thought you'd be happy to hear that my friends and I were voted Best Friends in the yearbook today.*

She wanted to tell her the good news, of course, but something else weighed on her. She sighed and got out of bed. Hidden in her desk drawer was her copy of the Canterlot High School yearbook from her freshman year. She opened it and looked at the photo of herself as Biggest Meanie. So much had changed since then. If only everyone could forget this about her past.

*After all,* Sunset began writing again in her journal, *if you hadn't forgiven me, I'd still be the arrogant student I was when I came here from Equestria without even saying good-bye to Princess Celestia.*

That was something she still felt bad about, too. What did Princess Celestia think of her? Did she know how much Sunset Shimmer had changed? Had she forgiven Sunset Shimmer, too? She crossed out what she'd written. There was no reason to burden Princess Twilight with all her regrets. Besides, there was so much good news to share.

*I hope you're having as great a week as I am,* she finished writing. *Your friend, Sunset Shimmer.*

She put her journal and pen on her night table, clicked off her light, and sighed. She always felt better after writing to Princess Twilight.

As Sunset drifted off to sleep, she didn't know that dark clouds were gathering over her house. She didn't see the sparks of magic flashing through the air. She didn't know that something was happening. Something terrible.

CHAPTER

5

# Not in the Picture

★ ★ ★

The sun was shining on the surf, and Twilight Sparkle was happily posing for a photo as her friends gathered around. A camera drone hovered in front of her and clicked. Twilight patted it. "Success!" she exclaimed, checking out the photo.

She had invented the best selfie device

ever! Now it would be easy to get a group picture of all their friends together. Except that the camera drone sputtered for some reason. Applejack looked worried.

"Your eyes do not deceive you," Twilight said confidently. "I finally invented a Selfie Sensing camera. It hovers into position whenever you want a selfie!" She wrangled the camera down to the sand as it tried to take off.

Applejack watched her struggle. "What was wrong with the old-fashioned way?" She mimed holding a camera at arm's length away from her.

Twilight Sparkle let go of her camera, and it stabilized, hovering in front of her. A sensor light turned green, a switch flicked on, and *click!* Twilight Sparkle posed just in time.

"The future's bright, Applejack!" she said happily.

The camera flashed. "Ah!" shouted Twilight. "Too bright! Too bright!"

Rarity had arrived with two blankets. "Which one should we use for the photograph?" she asked the other girls.

Rainbow Dash was confused. "You mean the white one? Or the white one?"

"This is toasted oat!" protested Rarity, holding up one of the blankets. "And this one is linen lamb's wool...." She pulled four more white blankets out of her shoulder bag. "Ivory cream, old lace, champagne, and, well, I suppose this one actually *is* white."

"Yeah," Rainbow Dash said with a laugh. "That's the one I'm talking about."

A gust of wind caught the blanket and whipped it into the air toward the ocean. Spike barked and chased after it.

"Don't worry, Rarity!" he called over his shoulder. "I got it!"

Pinkie Pie was headed toward the water, too, ready to splash in the waves. "No, I got it! I got it!"

"I got it! I got it!" Spike yipped.

A huge wave crashed over both of their heads, and they emerged from the surf soaking wet. The blanket floated out to sea.

"I don't got it." Pinkie sighed, disappointed.

"I don't got it," echoed Spike.

The blanket bobbed over a wave and suddenly started heading back toward them. A horrible raspy sound came from inside it.

"Ocean monster!" Pinkie screeched, splashing toward the shore.

A strange face emerged from underneath the blanket. It was Fluttershy wearing a mask and breathing through a snorkel!

"Quincy the sea turtle says there's some big waves coming that would be perfect for our picture," she told the others.

Sunset Shimmer saw all the girls getting into position as she hurried down the beach. This was a big moment for her. This was the yearbook photo she wanted everyone to remember. "All right!" she shouted to the others. "Who's ready to take a Best Friends photo?"

Twilight Sparkle whirled around and stared at her. She whispered something to Rarity, who shrugged. Applejack's eyes narrowed. Spike growled.

"What do you want, Sunset Shimmer?" Applejack asked.

Fluttershy twisted her hands nervously. "Please don't ruin our picture," she begged.

Sunset Shimmer laughed and went over

to join her friends. She noticed the camera drone. "Oh," she said, delighted. "You got the Selfie Sensor working, Twilight?" She posed with a big smile on her face.

The drone zipped away from her and hovered behind Twilight Sparkle. What was going on?

"Okay…" said Sunset Shimmer. Was she late? "Uh-oh, what did I do?"

Rainbow Dash crossed her arms defensively. "We're just trying to take a picture for the yearbook, okay?"

Sunset Shimmer agreed and nodded. "Should we do it now?"

None of the girls said a word. They all glared at her. Sunset Shimmer started to feel uncomfortable, but she had no idea what was the matter.

Applejack finally exploded, her face red.

"Sunset Shimmer? Asking to be in our Best Friends picture? Now I've heard it all!"

Sunset Shimmer looked from one girl to the other. "Am I missing the joke here?"

"The only joke," Rarity said through gritted teeth, "is whatever this is you're playing on us, acting all nice like you're our friend."

"And it's not funny!" cried Fluttershy, upset.

"Because you aren't nice," added Rainbow Dash.

"And we ain't friends." To make her point, Applejack linked her arm through Rainbow Dash's.

"Wait," spluttered Sunset Shimmer. She felt dizzy and strange. Everything was topsy-turvy. "What? Why?" She could hardly get out the words. Why were the other girls being so mean to her?

"You got applesauce in yer ears?" asked Applejack.

Sunset Shimmer touched the geode around her neck, and it glowed. It gave her the ability to read people's minds—if she touched them. She reached her hand out to Applejack.

What she saw devastated her. She saw herself as the she-demon, but she couldn't see herself apologizing to all the girls. She saw the Friendship Games but not the conversation she had with Twilight Sparkle about forgiveness. She saw everyone trying to save Twilight at Camp Everfree—except herself. She just wasn't in the picture. She jerked her hand away. She couldn't take it anymore. Why wasn't she in any of Applejack's memories?

"It's like I've been erased!" She shuddered.

All the slumber parties and games and laughter and jokes and friendship. All of it was gone. The only thing anyone remembered about her was that she was the Biggest Meanie.

CHAPTER 6

# The Worst
Nightmare Ever

★ ★ ★

Sunset Shimmer wriggled her toes in the sand. She could feel them. She could hear the waves crashing on the shore. She could feel the sun on her face. Still, this had to be a nightmare. It was a nightmare. "Wake up, Sunset," she told herself. "Wake up!"

*Ouch!* Pinkie Pie had pinched her!

"Nope," said Pinkie. "You're awake." She pinched herself. "*Ow!* Me too!"

Sunset Shimmer had to figure out what was going on. Maybe it was just something the matter with Applejack. Maybe she was erased from only Applejack's memory. She reached out to touch Rainbow Dash's arm.

She peered into Rainbow Dash's memories. There was the bike race at the Friendship Games when Sunset Shimmer had crashed and Rainbow Dash had rescued her...because they were friends. But that's not what was happening in Rainbow Dash's memory! Sunset Shimmer saw herself falling off her bike. She saw Rainbow Dash skidding to a halt and looking back at her. But instead, she saw Rainbow Dash shrug and get back into the race. How could that be?

"No!" Sunset Shimmer exclaimed. "Rainbow Dash, you saved me in that race!"

"What are you talking about?" asked Rainbow Dash.

"I can see your memories," Sunset Shimmer explained. "And I'm not in them."

Hearing this, Applejack looked concerned. "And exactly how is it that you can see our memories, if you don't mind me askin'?"

"With this!" Sunset Shimmer held up her geode necklace. Surely all the girls would remember their adventures together at Camp Everfree.

Rarity peered at the necklace. She shook her head. "It's obviously a cheap knockoff of ours."

"We got them together," insisted Sunset Shimmer. "You were there, remember?"

Pinkie whispered something to Rainbow Dash. Rainbow Dash shrugged.

"Why is she still talking to us?" wondered Fluttershy out loud

Sunset Shimmer ignored her and turned to Pinkie. "Pinkie Pie, what about when I came over to your sleepover before Battle of the Bands?"

"Ha!" exclaimed Pinkie, flabbergasted. "The closest you've ever come to a party of mine is freshman year, when you pretended to be Applejack and texted me: *Your party is lamer than a hungry duck in snow boots.*" Tears welled up in Pinkie's eyes at the memory of how hurtful that had been.

"Like I'd ever say that." Applejack reached out to Pinkie Pie reassuringly.

Pinkie's lip quivered. "It really hurt my feelings."

"And it wasn't very nice to ducks, either," added Fluttershy, glaring at Sunset Shimmer.

Sunset Shimmer felt hollow inside. "That was a long time ago," she whispered. She turned to Twilight. "You remember me, right?"

Twilight Sparkle shook her head.

"We've been through so much together," pleaded Sunset Shimmer. "Please..."

"I only met you once, when you yelled at me at the Friendship Games," Twilight answered.

"Doesn't anyone remember that I have changed?" cried Sunset Shimmer.

All the girls looked at her blankly.

But there *was* one friend who might remember her! Princess Twilight back in Equestria! "I'll be right back," she told the girls as she dashed across the beach toward home.

"Hurry back, darling!" said Rarity politely.

Twilight Sparkle's camera drone hovered in front of Rarity and snapped a photo.

"No, no, no!" protested Rarity. "This is my best side for my fake smile!"

The drone buzzed to her other side and clicked.

"Much better!" noted Rarity.

# CHAPTER

7

# Time for Homecoming

★ ✶ ★

Sunset Shimmer raced upstairs to her bed-room. She opened her journal and began writing an urgent message in it to Princess Twilight.

*This is going to sound crazy,* she scribbled as fast as she could, *but... are we friends?*

She hesitated, unsure if she should ask

her next question. *Am I nice?* she finally wrote.

She put down her pen and stared at the blank space in her journal. How long would it take Princess Twilight to answer her? What would she say? What would she do if Princess Twilight didn't remember how much she had changed?

She glanced over to her desk at the yearbook from her freshman year. Biggest Meanie.

"Please answer, please answer, please answer," she whispered to the magic journal.

Nothing. It was still blank. She ran her fingers across the paper as though that might help the words appear. Just as she was about to give up, she noticed the blank space sparkle! Princess Twilight was writing back to her.

*Of course we're friends!*

Sunset Shimmer breathed a huge sigh of relief.

*Are you okay?* continued Princess Twilight in the journal. *What's going on?*

Sunset Shimmer picked up her pen and wrote as fast as she could. *Kind of hard to explain. Might be easier in person. Well, not in person, so to speak...*

Sunset Shimmer had to talk to Princess Twilight. She needed her help more than ever. It was time for her to go back.

She raced over to Canterlot High and stood before the statue of the Wondercolt in front of the school. The statue was actually a portal between the two worlds—but most people didn't know that. As soon as the coast was clear, Sunset Shimmer approached it, took a deep breath, and stepped through it, whirling and swirling through different dimensions until she landed in Equestria.

It took her a moment to get used to having hooves again, but soon enough she was standing on all four legs and shaking her mane free. She was a pony again.

Her eyes lit up as she saw Princess Twilight trot toward her, but she stumbled when she tried to walk. She tried to reach out with her hooves and tumbled forward. "Oops!" she apologized. "I was trying to hug you!"

Twilight Sparkle smiled warmly at Sunset Shimmer. It was good to have her back— and there was so much to show her. But what was going on back at Canterlot High?

CHAPTER 8

# A Surprising Reunion

★ ★ ★

"This is bad, Sunset," said Princess Twilight back at her castle. "It's way beyond anything I've ever heard of. Although..."

"What?" asked Sunset Shimmer.

"I just had an idea." Princess Twilight thought hard. She knew a lot about both friendship and magic, but this was one of the hardest, most confusing problems she had ever faced. "You might not like this," she warned Sunset Shimmer.

"I'll do anything to get my friends back," Sunset Shimmer pleaded.

"There is one pony who might be able to help, but I don't know if you two want to see each other."

"Who?" blurted out Sunset Shimmer. A moment later, however, she knew exactly whom Princess Twilight was talking about. "Oh." Her face fell.

Long ago, Sunset Shimmer had been one of Princess Celestia's students, but she had been impatient for magical power and had stolen Princess Twilight's enchanted crown. She'd ended up at Canterlot High in the world of human beings to learn about friendship with Princess Twilight's help. She'd never been back to apologize to Celestia. But the time had clearly come.

Together the ponies approached the majestic entrance to Princess Celestia's castle. They walked down the hallway along the red carpet side by side. Sunset Shimmer was nervous, but she was glad Princess Twilight was beside her. Princess Twilight gave her a reassuring smile. At the very end of the room, sitting on her throne, was Princess Celestia.

Sunset Shimmer felt ashamed. As she bowed before Princess Celestia, she kept her eyes lowered. None of the ponies in attendance whinnied or neighed. Princess Twilight held her breath.

"*Sooo,*" began Princess Twilight, trying to lighten the mood. "You'll never guess who's back! Actually, maybe you can guess, because she's right here, but...um..." She paused and bent her head close to Sunset Shimmer. "Am I helping?"

Sunset Shimmer took a deep breath. No one at Canterlot High remembered how much she had changed—but she did. She knew she was different. She knew what she had learned about friendship. "Princess Celestia," she began in a low voice, "the last time we saw each other, I was your snide little pupil who betrayed and abandoned you."

"I wouldn't have said it *that* way." Princess Twilight was stunned at Sunset Shimmer's bold honesty. "What Sunset meant to say is—"

"I mean," interrupted Sunset Shimmer, "that I come before you a changed pony, humbly asking for forgiveness, guidance, and knowledge."

Princess Celestia's face was serene and unreadable. Sunset Shimmer had no idea what she was thinking. But she wasn't going to let that stop her.

"Or," she continued, "I can just go, and you never have to see me again."

Twilight was about to jump in, but no sooner had she opened her mouth than Princess Celestia silenced her with a cool stare. Princess Celestia gazed into Sunset Shimmer's eyes for a long time. Sunset Shimmer's heart beat fast, but she didn't look away.

At long last, Princess Celestia spoke. "I have missed you, Sunset Shimmer." A small smile turned up the corners of her lips.

"I'm so sorry!" Sunset Shimmer gushed. She was so grateful not to be turned away.

Princess Celestia nuzzled her reassuringly, and Sunset Shimmer was overcome with happiness. Princess Twilight was ecstatic, too. Now everypony was friends again!

That is, everypony in Equestria. There was still the huge problem back at Canterlot High. Why didn't any of the human girls remember how Sunset Shimmer had changed?

CHAPTER

9

# The Biggest Reader

## ★ ★ ★

The ponies strolled together through the castle, trying to figure out what might have happened at Canterlot High. "I am not familiar with the exact spell that could have erased your friends' memories," mused Princess Celestia. "But it sounds unmistakably like Equestrian magic is at work in your world."

Princess Luna nodded her head in agreement. "Indeed, the toilings of this nefarious enchantment could portend unimaginable catastrophe if left unchecked."

Sunset Shimmer sighed audibly. She still felt wobbly being back in Equestria. At Canterlot High, the princesses' counterparts were the principal and vice principal. It could all get so confusing. "I'm so used to hearing you tell the students not to park in the faculty lot," she tried to explain.

Princess Luna frowned. What a strange thing to say. "This *faculty lot* you speak of sounds like a place of great power."

Sunset Shimmer smiled. Well, it was at Canterlot High, but most of the people there had no idea about the power of pony magic.

Princess Celestia opened the door to her

royal library. "The answers you seek are here," she said.

Sunset Shimmer had forgotten what an enormous place it was. "There's got to be a million books in here—"

"I wish!" interrupted Princess Twilight. "But don't worry. You're looking at somepony who knows this place like the back of her hoof."

Without a word, Princess Celestia began walking away from them and toward the very back of the library.

"Where are you going?" asked Princess Twilight.

"To the restricted section," answered Princess Celestia.

Princess Twilight's eyes widened. She couldn't believe it! There were more books here than she knew about? "There's a reh... reh..."

"Breathe, Twilight," whispered Sunset Shimmer to her friend.

In the very back of the enormous library, behind stacks and stacks of books, were two palace guards. As Princess Celestia approached, they stepped aside to reveal a hidden iron gate. Princess Celestia drew forth a key and opened it.

The restricted section was almost as big as the library itself. It was packed with ancient books and dusty scrolls and strange magical artifacts protected under glass. Princess Twilight was thrilled. She tried to breathe, but she couldn't talk. She loved to read and study!

Sunset Shimmer smiled. "You sure you're up for helping me go through all this stuff?"

"Don't take this away from me!" Princess Twilight blurted out.

Sunset Shimmer burst out laughing. Her

Canterlot High calamity was the best thing that ever happened to Princess Twilight.

Princess Celestia led them to a large machine with lots of levers. "I should warn you," she advised the ponies, "the archive's mechanical catalog has not been well maintained."

Sunset Shimmer touched a dust-covered crank, and it broke off. A drawer full of faded cards listing the books fell onto the floor. This did not look promising. But Princess Twilight was undaunted.

"Guess we'll just have to read everything! Come on!" she exclaimed.

Sunset Shimmer met Princess Celestia's eyes, and they both smiled. Princess Twilight was galloping up and down the stacks, reading the titles of the books out loud.

"No way!" she shouted. "Can you believe

they have *Canterlot Cantabiles Volume Thirty-one*? You heard me! *Thirty-one!* Sunset, that's when the series gets good! And look! Over here! An original *Wendigo Weather Warning* from the pre-Equestrian era..."

Sunset Shimmer looked all around the enormous room. How long would it take to read all these books? And would any of them even have the answer to what had happened to her? She tried not to feel hopeless. At least Princess Twilight seemed up to the job.

CHAPTER

10

# Most Likely to Get a Clue

★ ★ ★

Sunset Shimmer stretched and yawned. She had just finished looking through another enormous, boring book about the history of Equestria. She closed it with a thud.

"Did you know," she told Princess Twilight, "that Chancellor Puddinghead tried to pass a law mandating Earth ponies drink carrot juice at every meal? I do. Now."

*"Awww,"* Princess Twilight said, smiling happily. "Sounds like you got to read all the fun books. We should probably take a break from looking...."

Sunset Shimmer sighed, tired and disappointed.

"Because," said Princess Twilight, about to burst from excitement, "I found something!"

Sunset Shimmer couldn't believe it. Princess Twilight pranced up and down the aisles. She levitated a large wooden box over to a table and pulled out a few scraps of old parchment. She arranged them carefully on the table like puzzle pieces.

"You are familiar with the *Seven Trials of Clover the Clever*?"

Sunset Shimmer tried to pretend as if she were. "Uh, obviously. But, uh, let's see how much you know about it."

Princess Twilight wiggled happily. "Well! First of all, these date back to before the founding of Equestria."

Sunset Shimmer knocked on the box. "I'll try not to break it." Almost immediately, she realized that Princess Twilight was not in a joking mood. "I'm kidding," she said.

"Look at this," said Princess Twilight. On one piece of parchment was a drawing of a strange gray obelisk. It stuck up into the air like a pointy tower.

"The Memory Stone," read Sunset Shimmer. "That sounds promising."

Princess Twilight shared everything she had found out. "It belonged to an evil sorceress who was practically invincible. With the Memory Stone, she could erase any memory from anypony. Even fragments of memories."

Sunset Shimmer thought out loud. "Fragments like…memories of me being nice?"

"Clover the Clever knew the sorceress had to be stopped," continued Princess Twilight. "And the Memory Stone had to be destroyed, so he chased the sorceress across land and sea. But every time he got close, the sorceress would erase his memory and escape. But he kept finding her."

"How?" Sunset Shimmer wondered.

"These scraps of parchment! He secretly wrote everything down so he'd know what had happened and where to go next, even as he constantly lost his memories. Like a trail of bread crumbs."

"That's clever!" Sunset Shimmer grinned. "No wonder he was called Clover the Clever!" She studied the scraps of parchment. On one of them was drawn what looked like a swirling portal. Clover the Clever was chasing the sorceress through it.

"What happened on the other side of this portal?" asked Sunset Shimmer.

But Twilight didn't know. "The last page is missing. Clover must've hidden it to keep anypony else from finding the Memory Stone."

Sunset Shimmer studied the portal. It looked familiar. It looked just like going through the Wondercolt.

Princess Twilight thought the exact same thing. "What if the Memory Stone ended up in your world?"

"And what if," Sunset Shimmer continued, "someone is using it to make everyone hate me again?"

"But *who*?" exclaimed Sunset Shimmer and Princess Twilight together.

That was the question.

Who would have the magical power and the motive to divide Sunset Shimmer from her friends?

CHAPTER 11

# Wiped Out

★ ★ ★

The tide was slowly going out at the beach, but the sun was still shining brightly. Pinkie Pie rolled over on her beach blanket. "We've been out here awhile," she commented. "Time to reapply!"

But instead of grabbing a tube of sunscreen, she reached into her bag and pulled out...a cupcake! She smeared the frosting over her arms and rubbed it in. The other girls barely noticed.

Twilight Sparkle looked out across the ocean, lost in thought. Something didn't feel right to her. "Should we be worried about Sunset Shimmer?" she asked at last.

"Yeah!" Trixie said with a laugh. "Worried she comes back!" She was reclining on a chair under an umbrella a little apart from the other girls. Snips and Snails fanned her with giant palm leaves. "I think it's a shame the way she's treating you, pretending to be your friend. She's obviously up to something. Sunset Shimmer thinks the whole school exists just to serve her." She snapped her fingers, and Snails handed her a bottle of water.

Trixie took a long drink. She cleared her throat to get the girls' attention again. "You know, seeing as how the yearbook president seems to be having a little identity crisis, I believe that means the vice president takes over. That's you, Rarity!"

Rarity shook her head. "If this is your way of asking to be made Greatest and Most Powerful in the Superlatives, the answer is no." Rarity suddenly felt very strange, as if she were about to get a headache. She rubbed her eyes. Maybe it was because the sun was so bright. "Didn't we have this conversation yesterday?" she asked the others. "I can't quite remember. It's all so fuzzy, like something's missing."

"Maybe we did, maybe we didn't," Trixie said with a shrug. "Memory is such a fickle thing. You never know when you'll forget something important. Like how Great and Powerful I am, which is why I need to be in the yearbook!"

Rarity rolled her eyes. Trixie just wouldn't give up. "I'll think about it," she said.

"That's all I ask," answered Trixie with mock sweetness.

She snapped her fingers again, and Snips and Snails resumed fanning her.

Rarity rubbed her forehead. She felt certain she was forgetting…something. If only she could remember what!

CHAPTER

12

# Best Sense of Humor

★★★

Back in Equestria, Sunset Shimmer and Princess Twilight were explaining to Princess Celestia what they had discovered about the Memory Stone.

"I should get back to my world," said Sunset Shimmer. "Maybe I can convince my friends I'm telling the truth, now that I know what we're looking for."

Princess Twilight levitated the scroll with

the picture of the Memory Stone into Sunset Shimmer's bag. "I'll stay here," she told Sunset Shimmer, "and search the restricted section top to bottom until I find a way to get your friends' memories back."

"If that's even possible." Sunset Shimmer sighed.

"Oh, it's possible," Princess Twilight reassured her. "I'll figure it out, even if I have to reorganize the whole library by subject, or maybe chronologically. Oh! And fix the broken catalog machine…" She caught sight of Sunset Shimmer's concerned expression. "I'll figure it out."

"Thank you," said Sunset Shimmer to Princess Twilight and Princess Celestia. "Both of you." Whatever happened at Canterlot High, Sunset Shimmer had regained a powerful friend in Equestria. It did her heart good to make amends at last with Princess Celestia.

Princess Celestia beamed at her. "This is quite a contrast from the last time we parted ways. With every choice you make, you prove yourself to possess a kind heart."

Sunset Shimmer blushed. "I guess I had a good teacher."

"You were a good student," said Princess Twilight, smiling.

Princess Celestia cleared her throat. "Are you saying I wasn't a good teacher?"

"No!" blurted out Sunset Shimmer.

"Oh, what I meant—" began Princess Twilight.

Princess Celestia chuckled softly, interrupting them. Relieved, they began laughing with her.

*Princess Celestia has a sense of humor?* thought Sunset Shimmer. *Looks like I'm not the only one who's changed.*

# Suspicious Activity

★ ★ ★

The girls were playing volleyball on the beach. That is, everyone except Applejack and Twilight Sparkle, who were sunning themselves nearby.

Rainbow Dash prepared to serve, narrating the game as she did. "It's been a grueling afternoon," she said in her best sportscaster voice, "but here we are at the final match. The next point wins! A hush falls over the crowd of ten thousand fans!"

Twilight began clapping. "Go, sports!"

"I'm not holding back this time!" Rainbow Dash warned the other team.

On the other side of the net, Fluttershy covered her eyes. "That's what I'm afraid of!"

"Bring it on, Rainbow Dash!" shouted Pinkie. "You and Rarity just bought your team a one-way ticket on the express train to *You're Going Down*!"

Rainbow Dash grinned, impressed. "Nice game face, Pinkie Pie."

"Thanks! I've been practicing all day." She giggled. She turned toward the drone camera. "Isn't that right, little baby camera? You're in my house now!"

The camera began beeping as if it were scared and darted behind Twilight. Spike growled at it.

"Somebody's jealous!" noted Rarity.

"Please call me when the flying can opener learns to fetch," barked Spike.

The drone whizzed out of view and returned a few minutes later with an open can of dog food!

Spike growled. "You're the worst." But when no one was looking, he gobbled up the food, licking up every last morsel.

Rainbow Dash served the volleyball. It arched over the net at top speed, and Fluttershy cowered, covering her head. But Pinkie Pie leaped up on top of her friend's shoulders and spiked the ball back over the net! Rainbow Dash dove into the sand to try to hit it back, but she missed. She sat up, brushing sand off her face, and saw Sunset Shimmer standing right in front of her.

"Great news, guys!" announced Sunset Shimmer. "I figured it out. Someone erased your memories with Equestrian magic! You don't remember, but we're still friends!"

Rainbow Dash spat out a grain of sand. Pinkie blinked, the sun in her eyes. No one said anything.

Sunset Shimmer pulled the parchment from her bag. "This is the Memory Stone," she told the girls. "Do you remember it?"

No one moved. It was as if all the girls were holding their breaths.

"Right," said Sunset Shimmer. "Guess not. But look, we *are* friends!" She took out her phone and began swiping through photos of all the girls together—playing music, doing one another's hair at slumber parties, teaming up at the Friendship Games, working together at Camp Everfree.

The girls peered at the photos. Could Sunset Shimmer have faked all these pictures? Why would she?

"Oh please!" Trixie said with a laugh, ignoring them. Snips and Snails were packing up her beach bag for her, trying to stuff in her enormous umbrella. "This is the same girl who made flawless fake photos of your friend trashing the gym," she reminded everyone.

Pinkie grabbed Sunset Shimmer's phone and studied the photos. She was outraged. "Yeah! Is this supposed to be me making such a ridiculous face? I'd never make a face like that!" Only she was. The exact same face. "Fake, I say!" she exploded.

Trixie cackled happily. "My work here is

done. Trixie *out!*" She threw a smoke bomb across the sand.

The girls coughed and rubbed their eyes. When the smoke cleared, Trixie was clambering over some rocks. "Don't forget, Rarity," she called out, "you promised to put me in the yearbook!"

"Wait!" called Sunset Shimmer. After all, she was still the editor in chief. "You did what?"

She was racing after Trixie when she tripped over Spike, her legs hopelessly tangled in his leash. She stumbled forward, and her foot crashed down, right on top of Twilight Sparkle's drone camera. *Crash! Crunch!* Catastrophe!

The camera sparked, buzzed, and fizzled. It was broken.

Twilight was furious.

"It was an accident! I can help fix it!" promised Sunset Shimmer apologetically.

"I think you've helped enough!" fumed Twilight.

All the girls glared at Sunset Shimmer. But Sunset Shimmer watched Trixie scurry away. She wondered where she was going. Somehow she had a feeling Trixie knew where the Memory Stone might be.

CHAPTER

14

# The Greatest and Most Powerful

★ ★ ★

The bell rang, and Sunset Shimmer closed her locker. Ever since she'd arrived in school, she'd noticed kids staring at her and whispering. Micro Chips approached her, trembling, and tried to hand her a wad of cash—as if she'd demanded the money. She gave it back to him, upset.

"I don't want your lunch money!" Sunset Shimmer shouted. "I'm not mean! Got it? I'm not mean!"

He ran from her as fast as he could, still terrified.

Everyone was more scared of her than ever. It wasn't just her friends who had forgotten how much she had changed. All the kids at Canterlot High still thought she was the Biggest Meanie. Down the hall, Trixie was getting her books at her locker.

"So..." said Sunset Shimmer, approaching her. "Here we are."

"Here we so are," agreed Trixie, not sure what she meant. "You really want to do this here in the hallway in front of everyone?"

Sunset Shimmer raised a single eyebrow. "Up to you." She was trying to control her temper.

Trixie smirked and reached into her locker. She pulled out a giant poster board. It was a mock-up of the Superlatives page of the yearbook, and there was Trixie under the headline *Greatest and Most Powerful!*

"Behold!" proclaimed Trixie. "Canterlot High School's Greatest and Most Powerful Student! If this doesn't convince you, I don't know what will."

"Where's the Memory Stone?" exclaimed Sunset Shimmer in exasperation. "You turned my friends against me just because I wouldn't put you in the yearbook as the Greatest and Most Powerful? Which isn't even an official Superlative!"

Trixie was genuinely baffled. "What are you talking about?"

"It is not a category!" shouted Sunset Shimmer.

"No," Trixie answered quickly, shaking her head. "What Memory Stone?"

Sunset Shimmer sighed deeply, trying to keep herself calm. "The one you used to erase everyone's memory, you manipulative...blowhard!"

Trixie barely noticed the insult. Instead she was thinking. "There's a stone that could make everyone forget all the bad tricks I've done...." She caught herself. "Which is *none*. Your puny rock pales in comparison to the Great and Powerful Trixie!"

Trixie struck a pose next to her poster and glanced at Sunset Shimmer hopefully.

"I don't believe it," murmured Sunset Shimmer. "You have no idea what I'm talking about."

"I don't," admitted Trixie. "Sorry."

Sunset Shimmer slumped against the

row of lockers. She didn't have another plan. She'd been so convinced it was Trixie who had cursed her.

"Did somebody really erase everyone's memories of you?" asked Trixie.

Sunset Shimmer nodded. A tear slipped down her cheek.

"So," said Trixie. "Even though we all know you're the Biggest Meanie, you're saying you're not mean anymore?"

"It's complicated," said Sunset Shimmer as she shrugged and sat down on the hallway floor.

Trixie took a seat beside her, thinking. Sunset Shimmer had no idea why she'd joined her. Kids passed them in the hallway. Some of them edged away when they saw Sunset Shimmer. A few kids caught sight of Trixie's poster and giggled to themselves.

At last, Trixie spoke up. "You have this idea of who you're supposed to be, but no one at school sees you that way, is that right?"

Sunset Shimmer smiled and nodded.

"Trust me," said Trixie, "I get it."

This was all really surprising. "I can't believe," admitted Sunset Shimmer, "that the only person who believes me is the one I called a manipulative blowhard." She extended her hand. "Sorry."

"I took it as a compliment," said Trixie with a toss of her head. And she meant it. "Let me help you find the Stone," she told Sunset Shimmer.

"What's in it for you?" Sunset Shimmer asked suspiciously.

Trixie grinned and pointed at her poster.

"No way," responded Sunset Shimmer.

"Absolutely not." No way would she give Trixie that Superlative.

"If you'd rather go on being the Biggest Meanie, that's fine by me...." Trixie grinned again at her. She was perfectly happy to give Sunset Shimmer time to think it over.

CHAPTER

15

# A Missed Message

★ ★ ★

Sunlight flooded the restricted area of the library in Equestria. Piled in front of Princess Luna and Princess Celestia on a large table were all kinds of books, scrolls, and parchments.

Princess Twilight was frustrated. "I've looked everywhere! Why can't I find the missing pages?" She banged her head on the table and knocked over the wooden box. It fell onto the marble tiles and broke into pieces. But there must have been a secret compartment in the box, because poking out between two pieces of wood was a scrap of parchment!

"This is the last piece!" exclaimed Princess Twilight. She studied the tiny piece of paper, and her eyes widened. "Clover the Clever buried the Memory Stone," she told the others. "The rock formation must be somewhere in the other world. But it doesn't say how to get your memories back."

Princess Celestia looked concerned as Princess Twilight turned the paper over. *"Perhaps,"* read Princess Twilight, *"if I had destroyed the Stone right away, some of my memories could have returned, but when the* sun sets on the third day after a memory has been taken, it is erased forever."

"You must warn Sunset Shimmer at once," said Princess Celestia, alarmed.

Princess Twilight immediately went back to her own castle to write in her magic journal.

But Sunset Shimmer had left her journal in her book bag in her locker. It buzzed and glowed, but Sunset Shimmer had no idea that Princess Twilight was trying to get in touch with her. She was too busy looking for the Memory Stone with Trixie.

"So where should we start, partner?" Sunset Shimmer asked Trixie.

"How about with 'What shall I call you?'" answered Trixie. "I'm thinking the Great and Powerful Trixie's pretty decent for an assistant-detective-helper person."

Sunset Shimmer smiled, and they walked through the main doors to explore the campus.

Far behind them, hidden in the book bag behind the locker door, the journal kept buzzing and glowing.

CHAPTER

16

# Best
# Detective

$$\bigstar \bigstar \bigstar$$

The girls were all sitting together in the cafeteria, and Pinkie Pie was making everyone laugh...about something. But Sunset Shimmer had no idea what it was. She was at a table all by herself. She looked at her lunch; she didn't feel like eating any of it.

Trixie slammed down her tray and then

plopped into a chair beside Sunset Shimmer. "A cafeteria full of suspects, two detectives, and one Memory Stone. Seems impossible, but so does pulling a rabbit out of a hat, and I do that all the time."

Fluttershy, overhearing her, swirled around in her chair, upset. What was Trixie doing to rabbits?

"Don't give me that look," said Trixie, noticing Fluttershy and shrugging. "They love it." She began crunching on her carrots, thinking the whole time about the case. "Let's talk motive. Who here hates you enough to erase everyone's good memories of you?"

Sunset Shimmer looked around the room, thinking back to freshman year. There were the kids she had bullied, the kids she had teased, the kids she had ordered around.

"If you go back far enough…everyone," she sighed.

Trixie pulled out a little notebook and wrote down what she said. *Known enemies: all.* There was only one option. They would have to question everybody in the whole school. She looked up at the clock, stuffed her sandwich into her pocket, and grabbed Sunset Shimmer. "C'mon," she urged. "No time to lose!"

Their first stop was the nurse's office. Bulk Biceps sat in a chair with a thermometer in his mouth. Nurse Redheart looked up as the girls stormed in. "Good afternoon, ladies," she said. "You feeling okay?"

Trixie whipped out her notepad and narrowed her eyes suspiciously. "That depends on how well you answer my questions. Has anyone come in complaining of memory problems recently?"

"Not that I can recall...." Nurse Redheart answered.

"You can't recall?" Trixie shook her head sadly. "We're too late!"

The next stop was the computer lab. Micro Chips leaped out of his chair when the girls entered the room. "Will you accept creamed toast?" he said, offering up his lunch tray.

"What?" Sunset Shimmer was so confused. "*Ew!* I told you I don't want your lunch money, and I definitely don't want your lunch."

"Speak for yourself!" said Trixie, glancing at Micro Chips's tray. "Word around school is, you know a lot about erasing memory."

Micro Chips nodded. "I erased a ton of memory just this morning."

"You did!" exclaimed Sunset Shimmer. A lead at last!

Micro Chips held up a hard drive. "Four terabytes of quantel-accelerflex memory to be precise."

The girls' faces fell. This was no good.

"How come no one's ever impressed by that?" Micro Chips wondered out loud. But the girls were already gone. They had more investigating to do.

When the bell rang, Sunset Shimmer and Trixie began cornering kids at their lockers and showing them the picture of the Memory Stone. No one recognized it.

"Is there anything you can tell us about it?" Sunset Shimmer asked Maud Pie. Pinkie Pie's sister was super smart. Maybe she would notice something about it. "Anything at all?"

"I can't tell much from a drawing," said

Maud Pie. "Only that it's felsitic intrusive igneous, granular in texture, most likely arranged in an equigranular matrix, with scattered biotite mica and amphibole, at least sixty-five percent alkali feldspar by volume, with a melting point of twelve-fifty centigrade, plus or minus ten degrees."

Sunset Shimmer's mouth fell open. Trixie was dumbfounded.

"Sorry I couldn't be more helpful," Maud apologized.

But that was the only lead they came up with, and they weren't even sure what it meant. Nobody else recognized the Memory Stone, or maybe, nobody else remembered it. They were stuck.

"Sure, it seems like we've only come up with dead ends," said Trixie. "But I mean, it could be worse."

Sunset Shimmer looked up and saw her old friends walking and laughing together. They were probably headed to the Sweet Shoppe…without her. Later, they'd text one another and share jokes and stories. She missed them. She missed them a lot.

"It is worse," she said very quietly. Losing her friends was the worst thing of all.

CHAPTER

17

# The Worst Case of Invisibility

★ ★ ★

Twilight Sparkle was tinkering with her camera drone, trying to fix it. She tightened a last screw and turned it on. *Beep! Beep! Beep!* It buzzed into the air, flying in loops around the girls.

"Good as new!" Twilight sighed, relieved.

"The Best Friends yearbook photo, number thirty-six A, attempt eight, take two!"

Sunset Shimmer peered through the window of the yearbook office, watching the girls strike a happy pose together. Trixie came up beside her, shaking her head.

"On three, everyone say, *'Best friends!'*" exclaimed Twilight. "One, two, three..."

*"Best friends!"* shouted the girls together.

Twilight checked the photo; it was perfect! She sent it to the yearbook.

In the yearbook office, Sunset Shimmer saw the photo arrive in her in-box. She opened the photo on the yearbook computer.

"Stop looking at that," ordered Trixie. "You're just going to wind yourself up. You can't think if you're wound up." Trixie paced back and forth in the office, pretty wound up herself. "Think, Trixie, think!"

Sunset Shimmer flipped through the pages of this year's yearbook on the table. Here were all her classmates. Which one would want to hurt her so badly? "Who are we missing?" she wondered out loud. "We've talked to everyone, from A to Z."

Trixie looked over her shoulder. "Wait." She'd noticed something. Or rather, she'd noticed that something was missing.

At the end of the students' photos was a small line of text, *Not pictured... Wallflower.*

Trixie furrowed her brow. "Wallflower? Who's Wallflower?"

"I'm right here, you know," said a quiet voice from the corner of the room.

Sunset Shimmer blinked. Sitting at a computer was the quiet girl she'd met just a few days ago, or rather, realized that she knew. What was it about her? Sunset

Shimmer always seemed to forget that she was there.

"Who are you?" asked Trixie before Sunset Shimmer could stop her.

Wallflower sighed. "I've known you since third grade."

Trixie's face brightened. "*Ahh!* I remember third grade. Not you specifically, but what a grade it was. The Great and Powerful Trixie debuted her disappearing frog trick! One of my best. You know, a lot of people don't know how much work goes into raising tadpoles."

Sunset Shimmer was just about to say something nice to Wallflower to cover for Trixie's not knowing who she was when she noticed a gentle glow from her bag. It was her magic journal! Princess Twilight was trying to get in touch with her. Maybe she had figured out what had happened to the Memory Stone and who had cursed her.

She picked up the journal eagerly. *Sunset, we think the Memory Stone was buried under this rock formation,* she read to herself. *And if you don't destroy the Memory Stone by the time the sun sets today, all those memories will be erased forever.*

Attached to the note was a picture of the rock formation. Sunset Shimmer felt more hopeless than ever. *How am I supposed to find a rock formation that looks like a rock formation?* she thought.

Except that right in front of her was another photo of the same rock formation. It was the screen saver on Wallflower's computer.

Very carefully, Sunset Shimmer slipped the journal back into her bag. She tried to keep as calm as possible. "Can I ask a silly question, Wallflower?" She hoped Wallflower didn't hear the tremor in her voice. "Where did you take that lovely photo?" She pointed at the screen saver.

"That's my garden," said Wallflower. "Well, the school's garden, technically. I'm the president of the Gardening Club. I founded it, too. I'm also the only member. And the only one who's ever been to the garden. Or seen it. Or even asked about it."

"You're not really into other people, are you?" asked Trixie.

Wallflower blushed. "I was maybe going to add this picture somewhere in the yearbook. What do you think?"

"Sorry, Sunset doesn't let anyone put things in her yearbook, no matter how much they deserve them," answered Trixie, pointedly.

"No, you should do that," Sunset Shimmer contradicted Trixie. "So don't let us keep you from working on it."

Trixie exploded. "What? The Great and Powerful Trixie is annoyed and insulted. Why does this random person you don't even know get to be in the yearbook, but your esteemed partner...?"

Sunset Shimmer waited and then shook her head softly to Trixie. When Wallflower's back was turned, she pointed at the computer. "A clue," she whispered.

Very quietly, Sunset Shimmer snuck up behind Wallflower. She needed to know what she was thinking. All she had to do was touch Wallflower's shoulder ever so lightly....

But Wallflower whirled around. "What are you—?"

Sunset Shimmer grabbed her by the wrist. There was no time anymore to be subtle. She had to know what was inside Wallflower's head. She saw flashes of life at Canterlot High. Students were hanging out in the parking lot and in the gym. There they were at the Battle of the Bands and at Camp Everfree. And there was Wallflower, always in the shadows and a step behind. "Hey, guys, wait for me!" she whispered. She was always the last one picked, the one that was overlooked, the invitation that never got sent, the one kid without a valentine. She was used to it. She expected it.

Sunset Shimmer saw Wallflower walking through the woods all by herself. She was unhappy, like she always was. She was lonely. She came to a clearing, and right in front of her was a strange triangular rock formation. That's when she first decided to garden. She began planting flowers and succulents and creating a garden. She dug in the dirt with her shovel to plant a baby tree, and the spade hit something hard. With her hands, she cleared away the dirt. Was it a treasure? Wrapped in cloth was what felt like a jewel. Wallflower unwrapped the package. It was the Memory Stone!

Sunset Shimmer saw Wallflower examining the cloth. Drawings on it showed a series of ponies learning how to use the Stone to erase memories. It showed a group of ponies with thought bubbles above their heads. Inside their thought bubbles was another pony. But in the next picture, all that remained inside the thought bubbles was an *X.* The other pony had vanished from their minds!

But the last thing Sunset Shimmer saw inside Wallflower's mind was the hardest of all. She saw herself. She was shutting down the yearbook office, turning off the lights and locking the door. She didn't notice that Wallflower was still in the room. She'd overlooked her again. Laughing, she left with her friends.

Wallflower stood in the dark by herself. Left behind again. "I'll just finish up in the dark by myself." She sighed. She sat down at a table and began flipping through an old yearbook. She was upset and grumbling to herself. "Why should you notice me? After all, you're Sunset Shimmer. Everybody loves you now."

Wallflower turned to the page in the old

yearbook where Sunset Shimmer was the Biggest Meanie. "Why can't they see you haven't changed?" she wondered out loud. That's when she remembered the strange stone she'd found.

Later that night, Wallflower crept out to the garden and dug up the Memory Stone again. She studied the instructions on the cloth. She closed her eyes and placed her fingertips on the magical object. The Memory Stone began to glow. A beam of light began to shine forth from within it. Wallflower kept her hands on the Stone.

The beam of light blasted through the forest, past the high school, and found its way right to Twilight Sparkle's bedroom. It shone on her forehead. A tiny spark emerged and floated out her window. The same thing happened to Pinkie Pie, to

Applejack, and to all the girls. The beam of light from the Memory Stone took away the spark that held all their nice memories of Sunset Shimmer. The sparks drifted through the nighttime sky under the stars. They found their way back to the Memory Stone. *Whoosh!* The Memory Stone stopped glowing. It had absorbed all the students' memories. Wallflower lifted her fingers off the Stone and opened her eyes. The curse was complete.

Sunset Shimmer let go of Wallflower's wrist. "You erased everyone's memories?"

Wallflower stared at her defiantly. "Yes."

"Wait, who are you again?" Trixie was confused.

CHAPTER

18

# Let's Forget This Ever Happened

★ ★ ★

This was the last straw for Wallflower. "I feel like I'm a ghost that nobody sees!" she exploded. "The trees, the plants—they're the only ones that notice me. But not you, never you, never somebody I actually go to school with and sit next to in class."

Sunset Shimmer was thinking fast. They

didn't have any time to lose. They had to find the Memory Stone fast—and Wallflower would have to take them to it. Sunset Shimmer glanced at Trixie, trying to be subtle. She nodded. Trixie immediately understood what she was saying. Sunset Shimmer began inching toward Wallflower's backpack while Trixie kept her attention.

Wallflower continued her tirade. "I'm always alone. Except for my shadow. And I don't even think you see that!" She didn't notice that Sunset Shimmer was sneaking past her.

"I'm invisible!" cried Wallflower dramatically. "It's like . . . like . . . like I don't exist."

Sunset Shimmer quietly unzipped Wallflower's backpack. Luckily, Wallflower didn't seem to hear her. She was too absorbed in what she had to say.

"I'm an empty book no one will ever read! Next to my name in the yearbook will just be a blank, a question mark, an empty space. No one's ever going to remember me, but will I ever forget how much it hurts to be ignored?" Nervously, Sunset Shimmer felt inside the last compartment of the backpack.

"I'm like a fading star at dawn," Wallflower moaned. "Invisible!"

Sunset's fingers touched something hard in the backpack. *The Memory Stone? It must be!* She was just about to pull it out when Wallflower stopped her and snatched away the backpack.

"What did I do to you?" Sunset Shimmer pleaded. "I don't even know you!"

"Exactly!" shouted Wallflower, furious. "You had everyone fooled, but now they know you're still the Biggest Meanie!"

Sunset Shimmer swiped the freshman yearbook across the table, startling everyone. Her eyes were blazing. "You're about to see how mean I can get!"

Trixie was startled. "Whoa, whoa! Let's not antagonize the person with the all-powerful mystery rock!"

Wallflower clutched the glowing Memory Stone. "I don't like confrontation," she hissed. "Let's just forget this conversation ever happened!"

She whispered something to the Stone in her hands. A beam of light shot out from it and zapped Sunset Shimmer right in the forehead. Another beam zapped Trixie. Their foreheads glowed. For a moment, it was as if they were watching themselves in reverse. Sunset Shimmer lunged for Wallflower, begging her for the Memory Stone, but it was too late.

Sometime later, Sunset Shimmer opened her eyes. She felt as if she was waking up after a long nap. Why was she in the yearbook office? What was Trixie doing beside her?

"What was I saying?" Trixie asked groggily. "I'm sure it was something brilliant." She rubbed her eyes and looked around the room. It was three o'clock. Where had the day gone? She staggered up and headed toward the door, but it wouldn't open. She jiggled the handle. The door was locked. How strange!

"What are we even doing in here?" she wondered out loud.

Poor Sunset Shimmer rubbed her head. It hurt as if she had hit it. There was something, something she was supposed to do, but she just couldn't think what it was. What was it?

"I don't remember anything," she whispered with a terrible feeling of dread.

CHAPTER

19

# A Magic Moment

## ✷ ✷ ✷

The school day was over, and most of the students had left the building. The athletes were on the field practicing. A few kids were hanging out, talking at their lockers. From far away down the hallway came the sound of yelling and pounding.

But no one walked past the yearbook

office. No one saw the door shaking. No one heard the banging.

"Is anybody out there?" called Sunset Shimmer, her voice muffled. "Somebody open the door!"

Trixie leaned back in a desk chair and watched Sunset Shimmer freak out. Sunset Shimmer shouted and banged, but nothing happened. Eventually exhausted, she collapsed onto the floor.

"If we don't get out of here and figure out who has the Memory Stone," she sighed, "in a few hours it will be too late to restore everyone's memories. I'll lose my friends forever!"

Trixie shook her head sadly. "Doesn't matter if we get out. How are we supposed to catch someone who can erase our memory every time we get close to catching them?"

But her words triggered something for Sunset Shimmer. Her eyes lit up, and she began thrusting her hands into her pockets. Even if she couldn't remember what it was, she knew there was something that she needed to look for. She pulled out a crumpled piece of paper.

The only way to catch someone with the Memory Stone was by being just like Clover the Clever! "Look!" she exclaimed to Trixie, holding up the piece of paper. "I wrote myself a note."

Trixie leaned in close. *"Check the video,"* she read out loud. She wrinkled her brow. That wasn't very helpful. What video?

But Sunset Shimmer had already spotted Twilight Sparkle's camera drone. It was plugged into one of the computers. A red light was blinking. Barely able to breathe with excitement, Sunset Shimmer picked it up to inspect it. "Yes!" she shouted with relief. "It's been recording this whole time!"

"Twilight's camera? What are you talking about?" wondered Trixie.

"I don't remember doing it," Sunset Shimmer explained. "But I must have realized our memories could get erased, so I pressed record at some point! I left a trail of bread crumbs so we could find our way to the Memory Stone!"

Trixie bit her lip with anticipation. Sunset Shimmer pressed play. The video began playing. Sunset Shimmer's face filled the screen as she adjusted the camera. She gave a thumbs-up sign. Everything was working according to plan.

"Clever!" nodded Trixie, clearly impressed.

"I can't take credit for the idea," said

Sunset Shimmer. Thank goodness she'd learned about Clover the Clever's ordeal.

On the video, Sunset Shimmer was slinking up behind Wallflower, who was editing her photo at her computer.

Trixie scratched her head, confused. "Who's that?" she asked.

"Wallflower," answered Sunset Shimmer.

"Name's not ringing a bell," Trixie said with a shrug.

The girls continued watching the video. Wallflower was going on and on about being invisible. Trixie rolled her eyes and pressed fast forward. They watched Wallflower talking super fast.

"She's got a lot to say, huh?" said Trixie. When Wallflower seemed to be done, Trixie took her finger off the button so the video could play at regular speed.

Sunset Shimmer confronted Wallflower. "What did I do to you? I don't even know you!" she was saying on the video.

"Exactly!" answered the recorded Wallflower triumphantly.

Trixie nodded. She'd just figured something out. But she needed to see more of the video to make absolutely certain that her hunch was correct.

On the video, Wallflower was shouting at Sunset Shimmer. "You had everyone fooled, but now they know you're still the Biggest Meanie!"

"You're about to see how mean I can get!" said Sunset Shimmer.

Trixie was surprised by Sunset Shimmer's anger. She pressed pause. "You know," she said, "she's kinda right about you."

"Thanks," Sunset Shimmer responded sarcastically.

Trixie cleared her throat. "Actually, the Wise and Moralizing Trixie was making a point." She gestured toward the video. "You said you didn't do anything."

"I didn't!" Sunset Shimmer was exasperated. "I wasn't mean to her at all!"

Trixie took a big breath. She'd had a big realization, but it would be hard to put it into words. She was sure she could do it. After all, she was pretty great and powerful. "Maybe," began Trixie, "it's not good enough to not be mean to someone."

Sunset Shimmer stared at her. She had no idea yet what Trixie was trying to get at.

"Maybe," Trixie continued, "you have to be nice."

Sunset Shimmer's mouth fell open in amazement. It was so simple and so obvious. But she'd never thought about it that way before. She nodded in agreement. "You're right."

"Always," Trixie said with a grin.

"Not that it matters," Sunset Shimmer sighed. "I'm still trapped in here. Unless you can magic us out of here?"

But Trixie's magic was mostly of the smoke-bomb variety—and it didn't exactly open locked doors. "What's the point in trying," she said, feeling defeated again. "You've seen enough of my tricks to know what'll happen."

Sunset Shimmer flicked through the photos on the camera drone. There was the picture of all her friends—all her ex-friends—taking their picture together. Not only wasn't she going to be in the yearbook with them, but after sunset they would never remember that they had ever been her friend. But she would never be as lonely as she had been before.

Sunset Shimmer smiled at Trixie. "At least when the sun goes down and everyone hates me forever, I'll still have one friend."

Trixie was surprised. Was Sunset Shimmer really talking about her?

"And I mean," added Sunset Shimmer, "she is the Greatest and Most Powerful Canterlot High School has to offer, so I guess I can't complain."

Trixie beamed, genuinely happy. Her eyes narrowed as she looked at the Best Friends picture. She had to do something for Sunset Shimmer. After all, they were friends.

"You poor fool!" she said to Sunset Shimmer. "You actually believed me when I pretended to give up? Mere stage banter! The Great and Powerful Trixie *never* gives up on herself…or her friends."

In a booming stage voice, Trixie announced, "Behold! The Magician's Exit!" She threw something into the middle of the room. It flashed, it popped, it smoked, and when the smoke cleared, Trixie was stunned to find herself out in the hallway. "It worked!" she exclaimed. "It worked! Yes! I finally did it!"

For the first time ever, Trixie had pulled off a real magic trick. She jumped up and down, she was so thrilled. Still, she needed to pull herself together. "Ahem," she said, calming down. "I'd tell you how, but a magician never reveals her secrets…."

There was only one problem. She was all alone in the hallway. Sunset Shimmer was still locked in the yearbook office!

"Still in here!" shouted Sunset Shimmer, banging on the door.

"*Umm,*" answered Trixie, stalling. "All part of the trick! I'll have you out in a jiffy!"

Trixie threw down another smoke bomb and wished with all her might that Sunset Shimmer might end up beside her. When the smoke cleared, Sunset Shimmer was in the hallway. Only problem: Trixie was back in the yearbook office!

"Know what?" yelled Trixie. "Leave me here! I'd rather be remembered as a martyr anyway."

"I owe you one, Trixie," said Sunset Shimmer. "I will never forget this!" She took off down the hallway.

"Never say never," sighed Trixie, still stuck in the room. If she'd learned one thing, it was how easy it could be to forget someone.

CHAPTER

20

# CurSed!

★ ★ ★

Sunset Shimmer looked everywhere for Wall-flower. Where could she have gone? The hallways were empty, no one was in the library, and everyone seemed to have gone home. Sunset Shimmer dashed out the front doors and scanned the parking lot.

Sunset Shimmer was so intent on looking

for Wallflower she didn't see the car headed right for her. *Honk! Honk!* Flash Sentry slammed on his brakes just as Sunset Shimmer jumped out of the way.

Sunset Shimmer shielded her eyes. The sun sank lower in the sky. At the very edge of campus, near the woods, she saw a figure running. "Wallflower! Stop!" yelled Sunset Shimmer.

Sunset Shimmer ran to catch up with her and passed her ex-friends all standing around Applejack's truck. But she had no time to try to explain to them what she was doing.

Wallflower behaved completely innocently as Sunset Shimmer approached her. "You remember my name?" she asked.

"I remember everything!" answered Sunset

Shimmer. "The Memory Stone! How I acted, all of it."

Wallflower's face turned red. "What? How? I erased the whole afternoon!" she shouted.

"Listen," begged Sunset Shimmer, trying to catch her breath. "I used to be just like you. Sure, I was popular, but I was lonely."

Wallflower couldn't believe it. "You're nothing like me, and I'm not lonely. I have my plants!" She cleared her throat. "That sounded less lonely in my head."

Applejack and the other girls watched them. Wallflower blushed, realizing they were listening.

"I'm sorry, Wallflower," apologized Sunset Shimmer.

"No, you're not," Wallflower insisted. "You're just trying to look good in front of your friends. And it's working! *Arrrgh!* How am I supposed to get back at you if nothing I do matters? *I hate you!*"

Sunset Shimmer winced and dropped her head.

The other girls were confused. What was going on? Sunset Shimmer was behaving so respectfully, but Wallflower seemed kind of out of control. Fluttershy covered her bunny's ears so he couldn't hear all the mean words and shouting.

Wallflower reached into her backpack. In her hands was the Memory Stone. "I wanted to teach you a lesson by erasing your friends' good memories of you," she told Sunset Shimmer. "But obviously that didn't work. But what if I erased *all* their memories of high school?" Wallflower grinned maniacally.

"You can't," pleaded Sunset Shimmer. "You'd be stealing their memories of one another!"

It was one thing for the girls not to remember their friendship with her, but what would it mean if they lost all thoughts of their wonderful adventures together?

The Memory Stone glowed. Wallflower held it tightly and closed her eyes. She concentrated.

Twilight was scared. Her eyes were on Wallflower.

"They won't be friends anymore," Sunset Shimmer cried.

Wind swirled around Wallflower. The Stone glowed brighter and brighter. The sun was lower than ever on the horizon. What could Sunset Shimmer do? She had no idea.

Wallflower cackled with glee. "They'll

think of one another the way you think of me, which is *not at all*!"

*Zap!*

A beam of light shot out of the Memory Stone.

*"No!"* cried Sunset Shimmer, hurling herself in front of it. White light surrounded her. "I ruined their friendship once before. I'd rather give up my own memories than let it happen again!"

Memories poured out of Sunset Shimmer. A tiny spark with a ghostly image of Fluttershy emerged from her forehead.

*"Argh!"* Sunset Shimmer screamed. "Fluttershy! No!"

Another spark flew out of Sunset Shimmer's forehead. It was a ghostly Applejack. Sunset Shimmer could feel her leaving. "No! No! No!"

Sunset Shimmer fell to her knees, stricken. It was one thing for all her friends to forget her, and something so much more terrible for her to lose her memories of them. Tears poured down her cheeks as the memories vanished. Another spark emerged. It was Rarity.

"Rarity!" shouted Sunset Shimmer.

What was happening? The girls watched Sunset Shimmer's ordeal without understanding it. Why was she calling their names? Why was she so upset? Did she care about them all this much?

Sparks of Rainbow Dash and Pinkie Pie left Sunset Shimmer. Her eyes fluttered. It was too much for her. It hurt her heart. "Pinkie Pie! Good-bye, Pinkie Pie! Good-bye, Rainbow Dash!"

Pinkie's eyes filled with tears. Something terrible was happening.

But the hardest memories to lose were the last ones. "Oh no, Twilight Sparkle," realized Sunset Shimmer, as scenes of their times together gathered into her mind. "You taught me everything I know about friendship. Don't forget me! Please! Don't forget me! *ARGH!*"

Twilight watched in horror as the beam of light from the Memory Stone crackled and zapped around Sunset Shimmer. *Whoosh! Whoosh! Whoosh!* Sparks flew. More and more memories left Sunset Shimmer.

Sunset Shimmer gasped for breath, dizzy. She looked all around her, confused. "This isn't Equestria," she said, rubbing her eyes. "Where am I? Princess Celestia?"

Twilight shuddered. Fluttershy covered her face. Pinkie started sobbing. Applejack and Rainbow Dash glared at Wallflower.

Wallflower wouldn't look at anyone. She kicked at the dirt with her shoe defiantly.

Sunset Shimmer stared at her hands. She wiggled her fingers and freaked out. "What's happened to me?" she cried. "Somepony help me!"

CHAPTER

21

# The Magic of Friendship

★ ★ ★

The shadows were long. The sun had almost set. Sunset Shimmer closed her eyes, shivering. She opened them again, and all the girls were staring at her.

"Who are you?" she asked.

Twilight stepped forward. "We are your friends," she announced.

Sunset Shimmer's face was blank. She didn't recognize her. But it didn't matter. The other girls crowded close.

"We may not remember you—" Applejack began.

"But after seeing what you did—" interrupted Pinkie.

"The sacrifice you made for us—" Rarity gushed.

"We would be proud to call you..." said Flutterfly.

"Our friend!" said all the girls together.

Twilight held out her hand to help Sunset Shimmer to her feet. As soon as their hands touched, however, the geodes around their necks began to glow. A sizzling line of energy crackled down Sunset Shimmer's arm and up Twilight's. Rainbow Dash reached out and took Twilight's hand,

and the energy traveled into her. Her geode glowed. All the girls linked hands, and all their geodes glowed. They were lifted into the air.

There was magic more powerful than the Memory Stone.

"Wallflower!" announced Twilight from high above her. "You have magic you do not understand, but it is nothing compared with the Magic of…"

"Yeah, yeah, yeah," Pinkie Pie interrupted. "We get it! Light her up, ladies!"

Just as the last rays of sunshine slipped below the horizon, a rainbow beam of magic color shot out of their circle and blasted the Memory Stone! It cracked. It *exploded*, sending sparks in all directions! It was like a Fourth of July fireworks show! *Kaboom! Kapowee! Hisssssss!*

Sparks flew onto the girls' foreheads as their memories rushed back to them.

*"Aaaaaah!"* screamed Sunset Shimmer.

*"Ohhh!"* cried Fluttershy.

"No!" yelled Wallflower.

"Yes!" exclaimed Pinkie.

Sunset Shimmer looked around her. "Twilight Sparkle?" she asked hesitantly.

"Sunset Shimmer!" cried Twilight, hugging her friend.

Pinkie Pie piled on, and they all shared a big group hug.

"We're so sorry," said Twilight at last.

"I'm just glad to have you all back," Sunset Shimmer told her.

Wallflower felt ashamed watching the reunion. Nothing had worked out the way she had imagined, and now she felt worse than ever. "I'd rather be invisible or forgotten than remembered as a villain," she whispered.

Sunset Shimmer broke apart from her friends and went over to Wallflower. After all, she knew a little something about making mistakes. "We've all been villains to someone at one time or another," she told Wallflower. "What matters are the choices you make today."

Wallflower looked down at the last shard of the Memory Stone in her hand. "When I first found the Memory Stone," she admitted, "I only erased little things—awkward hellos, saying the wrong thing, literally any public speaking...."

Twilight nodded sympathetically. She understood. "I've had plenty of awkward moments I wish I could erase, too."

"But it's no excuse," said Wallflower. "I'm

sorry for everything. I was so used to erasing memories that I got completely carried
away."

"It's okay," Sunset Shimmer said with a
smile, forgiving her. "I'm sorry, too. I may
have stopped being mean, but a great and
powerful friend helped me realize I still
wasn't very nice to you."

The other girls nodded in agreement.

"None of us were," agreed Applejack.

"And I know how hard it is being shy,"
offered Fluttershy.

"Everyone matters, Wallflower," Sunset
Shimmer said to her. "No matter how insig-
nificant or invisible they feel."

Wallflower took Sunset Shimmer's hands
and squeezed them. Somehow everything
had worked out in the end. Wallflower never
wanted to forget this moment. Not ever.

CHAPTER

22

# Most Improved

★ ★ ★

Sunset Shimmer was writing in her journal to Princess Twilight Sparkle. Not only was everyone friends again—but now the girls had a new friend, too.

*Dear Princess Twilight,* wrote Sunset Shimmer. *You can add a new ending to the archives. The Memory Stone is no more.*

Sunset Shimmer had wanted to write to Princess Twilight for a few weeks, but she'd been so busy getting the yearbook finished. Just that afternoon, a truck had arrived at Canterlot High with the finished books. Before the boxes could be unloaded, however, Vice Principal Luna had stormed out of her office, shouting, "No student parking in the faculty lot."

The faculty lot was a very powerful location. Sunset Shimmer smiled, remembering her trip to Equestria. Without the curse of the Memory Stone, she might not have gone back so soon.

*Thank you for your help,* she wrote to Princess Twilight. *Give my best to Princess Luna and Princess Celestia. I am happy to say that everything is back to how it used to be.*

Only that wasn't entirely true. Things were better than they had ever been.

CHAPTER

23

# Memories to Treasure

# ✷ ✷ ✷

Sunset Shimmer was hurrying to class the next day when Trixie stopped her in the hallway. She was waving her yearbook in the air.

"I demand to speak to the yearbook president!" she exclaimed.

Sunset Shimmer stopped, stunned. What was the matter?

Trixie flipped open her yearbook. "How did this get in here?" she demanded to know.

Among all the usual Superlatives was a giant photo of Trixie under the caption *Greatest and Most Powerful*. It looked just like the mock-up poster Trixie had created long ago.

Sunset Shimmer shrugged, pretending to be clueless. "A yearbook president never reveals her secrets!" She waved her hand like a magician she knew.

Sunset Shimmer peeked through an open door into a classroom. "I've got a delivery for Best Gardener!" she called out.

In the classroom, Wallflower was teaching Snips and Snails about pruning bonsai trees. She looked up and went over to Sunset Shimmer. There in the Superlatives was a picture of her! Not only that, her yearbook was filled with messages and signatures—from Sunset Shimmer, Fluttershy, Twilight Sparkle, and all her many new friends.

"You coming to lunch, Wallflower?" Sunset Shimmer asked her.

Wallflower nodded as she waved good-bye to Snips and Snails. Together, the girls headed off down the hallway.

At lunch they sat down with all the girls who were just discovering the biggest surprise of all in the yearbook: The photo on the beach of all the friends together included Sunset Shimmer. Twilight's camera drone had nailed the shot! It was perfect. But, on the opposite page, flexing his muscles, was Bulk Biceps.

"Oh come on, seriously?" complained Rainbow Dash, laughing.

Sunset Shimmer burst out laughing as the girls discovered her little joke.

It was so much fun to have good friends—and she never, ever wanted to forget how much they all meant to one another.

# THe yearBook Committee

It's time to help Sunset Shimmer
put together this year's Canterlot High
yearbook! Everyone needs to have his or her
photo taken on Picture Day. The students need
to create their own special pages, with quotes
and memories from the school year.
The Superlatives have to be voted on and
photographed. Help your friends be part of
a year to remember!

**What special skills and talents do *you* have to
help out with the yearbook?**

_____

_____

_____

_____

_____

# CLASS PICTURE DAY!

The girls are in a hurry to get ready for their close-ups! Can you match each girl with the accessory that best suits her style?

Sunset Shimmer

Rarity

Twilight Sparkle

Rainbow Dash

Applejack

Fluttershy

Pinkie Pie

cowboy boots

hair bow covered in sparkles

butterfly barrette

black leather jacket

skinny necktie

gauzy purple scarf

wristband

Which of the girls shares your sense of style?
How would you imitate her style in your photo?
List three things you are going to wear just like her!

My style is like ....Fluttershy....

I am going to wear:

1. ...Pink skirts.............

2. ...white boots...........

3. ...butterfly headbands

# Vote for your Friends!

Which of your friends would you pick for each of these Superlatives? Draw their picture or paste photos in the appropriate squares:

Class Clown

Me

Shiest

Best Dressed

# PHOTOSHOP

Pick the best photo for the Best Friends Superlative! Which one captures the Magic of Friendship? Circle your favorite

# a Wallflower Makeover

There's nothing like a little color to help a girl stand out from the crowd! Give Wallflower the sparkle and shine she needs to be unforgettable.

# CANTERLOT STUDENT PAGE

Every student lists their clubs and chooses
a favorite quote for their page!
Design your own page for the yearbook!

**Clubs:**

.......................................................

.......................................................

.......................................................

**Favorite quote:**

.......................................................

.......................................................

.......................................................

# LAUGH TRACKS!

With your own funny words, find out what
really happened to Clover the Clever!

**The** _Pink_ **Trials of Clover the Clever**
   *(adjective)*

The Memory Stone belonged to a _dirty_ sorceress
                              *(adjective)*
who was practically _glimmering_. With the Memory
                     *(adjective)*
Stone she could _jump_ any memory from
                 *(verb)*
anypony. Even _Canada_ of memories. Clover the
               *(noun)*
Clever knew the sorceress had to be _run_
                                     *(verb)*
and the Memory Stone had to be destroyed, so

he _bite_ the sorceress across _school_
    *(verb)*                     *(noun)*
and _Hollywood_. But every time he got close, the
     *(noun)*
sorceress would erase his memory and escape. But

Clover the Clever secretly wrote down everything so

he'd know what had happened and where to go next,

even as he constantly lost his _mom_. Like a trail of
                                *(noun)*
_dads_.
*(plural noun)*

# TREASURED FRIENDSHIP MEMORY

Quick! Someone has the Memory Stone!
Write down a memory that you never ever want
to forget! If you put it here, it can never be lost!

\* \* \*

_____

_____

_____

_____

_____

_____

_____

_____

_____

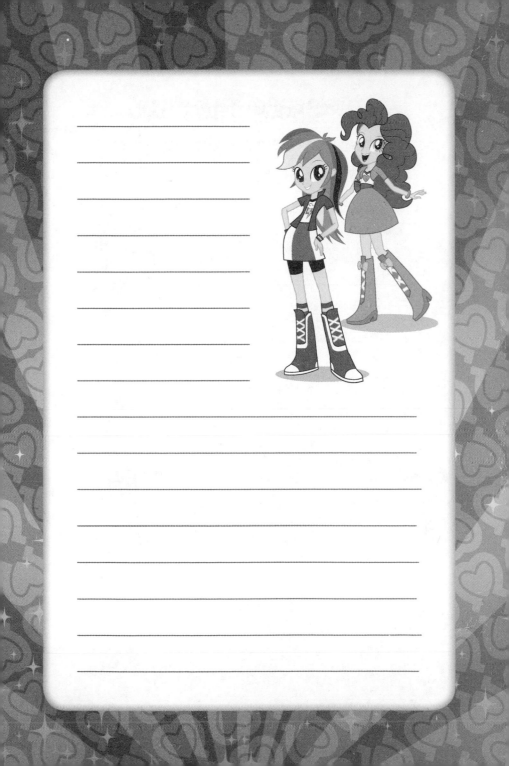

# INVISIBLE FRIENDS

Have you ever felt invisible like Wallflower?

Where were you? What happened?

_____

_____

_____

_____

_____

_____

_____

_____

_____

_____

_____

Think of someone at your school who gets overlooked sometimes. Is there someone who gets left out or picked last? What can you do to help this person feel included?

_____

_____

_____

_____

_____

_____

_____

_____

_____

_____

# autographs!

Sign your name in your friends' yearbooks!
What do you want to say to each special
friend from Canterlot High?

Sunset Shimmer

*jason zhang*
*cool jacket!*

Twilight Sparkle

*jason zhang*
*your'e a*
*genius*

**Rarity**

jaxom zhang

nice

hairdo!

**Rainbow Dash**

jaxom
zhang

 love your

Sonic

Rainboomz